DORA the EXPLORER

P9-BYQ-155

DORA saves the SNOW PRINCESS

adapted by Phoebe Beinstein   illustrated by Dave Aikins

SIMON AND SCHUSTER/NICKELODEON

Based on the TV series *Dora the Explorer* as seen on Nick Jr.

SIMON AND SCHUSTER
First published in Great Britain in 2008 by Simon & Schuster UK Ltd
1st Floor, 222 Gray's Inn Road, London WC1X 8HB
A CBS Company

Originally published in the USA in 2008 by Simon Spotlight,
an imprint of Simon & Schuster Children's Division, New York.

A CIP catalogue record for this book is available from the British Library

ISBN: 978-0-85707-425-6
Printed in China

10 9 8 7 6 5 4 3 2

¡Hola! Today I'm reading a book to all my friends. Do you like books? We love books! Boots, Tico, Benny, and Isa really want to hear a story about a snow princess, a witch, and a snow fairy. Can you see a story like that?

Once upon a time there was a little girl named Sabrina who loved snow. Sabrina lived in a lonely, dry forest where it never snowed. One day during a walk, she saw a little white dove sitting in a tree, crying.

"What's wrong?" Sabrina asked the dove.

"I'm caught in a trap set by a mean witch, but no one will free me because they're all afraid of her." The dove showed Sabrina his trapped foot.

"I'll free you!" said Sabrina, and she helped him out of the trap.

"You are very kind and brave," the dove said. "You must be the one! Follow me. I have something special to show you." The white dove led Sabrina to several bushes. "It's behind the bush with the purple berries," said the dove.

Sabrina looked behind the bush and saw something beautiful sticking out of the ground.

"It's a magic crystal!" the dove said. "Now look into it and smile."

So Sabrina did, and the most amazing thing happened.

It started to snow! Then Sabrina became the Snow Princess and the white dove became the Snow Fairy.
"Me, a princess?" Sabrina asked.

"Yes. The forest was under the Witch's spell, but because of your bravery and kindness all the snow animals are free!" said the Snow Fairy.

Everyone in the forest was very happy, until one day the Snow Princess saw the Witch flying in the sky. The Witch suddenly swooped down and grabbed the crystal out of the Snow Princess's hand. She made a mean face into the crystal to stop the snow, and then locked the Snow Princess in the top of a tower.

"Now it will never snow again. Ha! Ha! Ha!" said the Witch before she flew away.

The snow in the forest began to melt. The animals looked
for the Snow Princess, but they didn't see her anywhere, so
they asked the Snow Fairy to find her. The Snow Fairy knew
he didn't have much time before everything melted.

Look! The Snow Fairy is flying right out of the story!
He thinks I'm the Snow Princess!
Hi, Snow Fairy! I'm not the Snow Princess, but I think we can
help you find her because we know where she is - in the tower!
Let's jump into the book and help the Snow Fairy find her.
Are you ready to jump? Jump, jump, jump!

Now we need to find out where the tower is. Who do we ask for help when we don't know which way to go? Yeah, Map! Map says we need to go across the Icy Ocean, past the Snow Hills, and through the cave. Then we'll reach the tower.

I can see the Icy Ocean down this big hill. Benny's pulling a sledge that we can ride on.

Oh, no. I see that sneaky fox, Swiper. He's going to swipe the Snow Fairy! Quick, say "Swiper, no swiping! Swiper, no swiping! Swiper, no swiping!"

Good job! You stopped Swiper.

Here we are at the Icy Ocean, but we need a boat to go across. Look, there's the Pirate Piggies' ship! We love the Pirate Piggies. Will you help us call them? Say "Pirate Piggies!"

They're coming to help us. Let's get on their ship! Watch out for icebergs!

Look! That iceberg isn't an iceberg. It's an icy sea snake coming right towards us! The Witch must have done this. But the Pirate Piggies know just how to scare an icy sea snake. All you have to do is yell "Arrrrrrg!" really loud. Will you be a pirate and help us scare the snake? Ready? Yell "Arrrrrrg!" Wow, what a great pirate you are!

Yay! The Pirate Piggies got us across the ocean and we found a snow hill, but Boots says this snow hill is moving. Wait . . . this isn't a snow hill. Snow Fairy says that the Witch turned the hill into a polar bear! Does the polar bear look happy or angry? Angry? Uh-oh. We'd better run!

There's a girl with a dog sledge. Maybe she can help us!
Her name is Paj. Paj says she can take us away from the
polar bear and right to the cave.

Wow, Paj's dogs run fast! To get around the hills, we have to lean. Will you lean left? Great! Now let's lean to the right. Good leaning! Paj and her dogs helped us get away from the polar bear and brought us to the cave.

This cave is really dark. Can you see a way out? Yeah, up there! Let's climb up and out.

Now we can see the tower and the Snow Princess! But first we have to pull down the drawbridge to get to her. Snow Fairy is trying to fly to the switch, but since he's almost melted, he can barely fly. He might fall in the moat filled with crocodiles! We need to help Snow Fairy fly! Will you help Snow Fairy fly? Flap your wings! Flap, flap, flap! You helped the Snow Fairy! Nice flapping.

Snow Fairy was able to fly all the way to the switch and we reached the Snow Princess. She says the Witch put a spell on her and now she can't smile. If she can't smile into the crystal then it won't snow and everything will melt.

I can see the Witch coming now! Maybe I can pretend to be the Snow Princess and smile into the crystal. You can help me smile too.

Now I look just like the Snow Princess! The Witch thinks I'm the princess and that I can't smile, but do we have a surprise for her! We'd better hurry before everything melts. Will you help me smile into the crystal? *¡Uno, dos, tres!* SMILE!

We did it! Our smiles made it snow again, and the Witch lost her powers forever! Now the Magic Snowy Forest is safe!

The Snow Fairy dressed us all like princesses and princes. But anyone can feel like a prince or a princess if they're kind and brave and like to help friends! Thanks for being kind and brave and helping us. *¡Adiós!*